Charlie

This series is for my riding friend Shelley, who cares about all animals.

ISBN-13: 978-0-545-07933-4
ISBN-10: 0-545-07933-0

12 11 10 9 8 7 6 5 4 3 2 1 8 9 10 11 12 13/0

Printed in the U.S.A.
First Scholastic printing, October 2008

Charlie

Tina Nolan
Illustrated by Sharon Rentta

SCHOLASTIC INC.
New York Toronto London Auckland Sydney
Mexico City New Delhi Hong Kong Buenos Aires

ANIMAL MAGIC

Meet the animals

Visit our Web site at
www.animalmagicrescue.net

Working our magic to match the perfect pet with the perfect owner!

Animal Magic Open House!

Saturday, August 5th
Come and meet the animals looking for a new home!

Soccer star **Jake Adams** will be here to sign autographs at 2 P.M.!

APACHE

Seven-year-old piebald, 13.1 hands, Apache is looking for a keen rider who will ride him out in company or alone.

LIBBY

We don't know Libby's age, and she won't look her best until her clipped fur grows back . . . but she'll love you to pieces!

NEWS

CONTACT

RESCUE CENTER

in need of a home!

SATIN

A beautiful five-year-old Siamese who would like you to pamper her. She needs to be an only pet.

PENNY

A two-year-old border collie cross with lots of energy. Can you play ball with her and give her all the walks she needs?

BECKS

A four-year-old Great Dane and a friendly giant! He needs a very special home with plenty of room to stretch his legs.

KITTENS!

Our adorable litter is ten weeks old. You'll fall in love with Treacle, Snap, and Wilma the moment you see them!

Chapter One

"'Animal Magic — we match the perfect pet with the pefect owner!'"

Eva Harrison read the words on the computer screen. "You skipped the *r* in the second *perfect*," she pointed out to her brother, Karl. They'd been working together for almost an hour, designing a flyer for Animal Magic's Open House.

Karl added the *r* and scrolled through the rest of the flyer. "Can I print it out now?" he asked.

"Just a minute." Eva read the whole thing one last time. "'We take in and care for unwanted animals and place them with caring owners.' Yep, cool. 'We make sure that no healthy animal is ever put to sleep.' Yeah, that's good. 'In our first year we placed 124 dogs and 156 cats. We also found new owners for 5 horses, 2 goats, plus 42 rabbits and 13 guinea pigs.'" She looked at the photos underneath. There was one of three feral kittens, Treacle, Wilma, and Snap, and another of a white rabbit named Pom-Pom. "Cute!" she murmured.

"So can I print it?" Karl asked impatiently.

"Wait!" Eva read on. "'Animal Magic Open House. Saturday, August 5th. Meet a celeb!' This is the best part! 'Soccer star Jake Adams will be here to meet you on

Saturday at 2 p.m. Jake and his girlfriend, Marietta, are big fans of Animal Magic, so don't miss your chance to meet them and get Jake's autograph!' Can you believe it?"

"I know, this really is cool!" Karl agreed, tapping keys to begin printing the flyers. He and his best friend, George Stevens, were seriously into soccer. "I can't wait to meet Jake!"

"I already have," Eva reminded him. It wasn't often that she was one up on her older brother, but this time she was. "I was with Dad when he took Charlie to Jake's house, remember."

"Yeah, no need to rub it in," Karl muttered, keeping an eye on the printer as it churned out the flyers.

Eva sailed on regardless. "Jake lives at Okeham Hall, a massive mansion with a

swimming pool. He came to the door with Marietta. I handed him Charlie, and he said thanks. He said we were doing a great job."

"Yeah, yeah!" Karl sniffed. "Next you'll be telling me that it was you who persuaded him to come to our Open House!"

"Yeah, well, no. Actually, it was Dad." Eva had to admit the truth. "Jake invited us in. That was when Dad asked him to be our last-minute celebrity guest. Jake said he'd love to do it if it helps to raise our pro-feel–"

"Raise our what?" Karl cut in.

"Pro-feel. You know, if it helps make us more well known."

"You mean *profile*!" Karl grinned.

"Whatever." Taking a stack of flyers fresh from the printer, Eva blushed and made a quick exit. "Only two days to go!" she

muttered. "I'd better put these in every mailbox in town."

"Here, take another *peel*!" Karl laughed. "And remember, take it easy. Delivering those flyers means you'll have to walk *meels* and *meels*!"

"Ha!" Eva retorted, taking off for the vet clinic to find their mom.

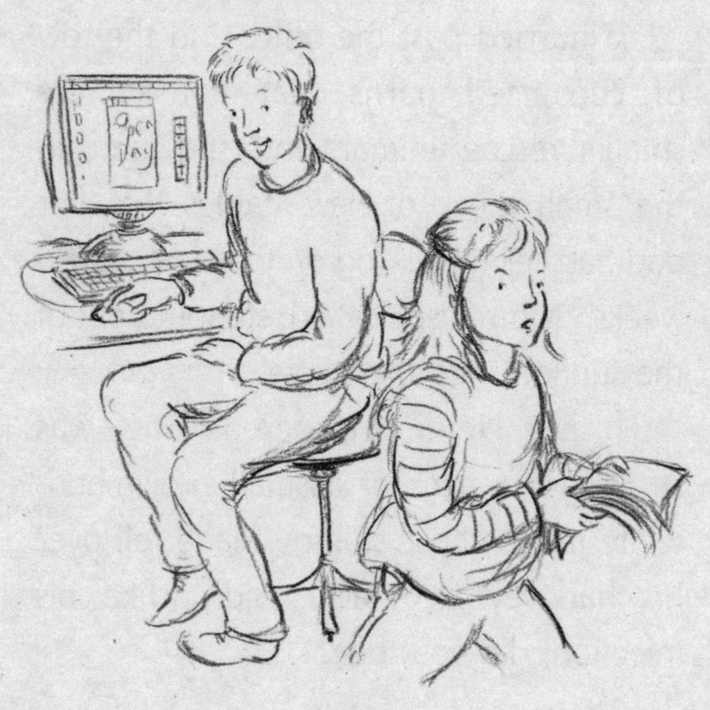

"Hi, Dad. Is Mom around?" Eva asked, popping her head around the office door. "Is she in the examining room?"

Her dad looked up from his pile of papers. "She's in the stables, vaccinating the two ponies we brought in yesterday."

Eva hurried past the office and the row of converted barns that housed the smaller rescue animals until she came to the small block of new stables that her dad had been working on for the past few weeks. "Mom?" she called, stepping out of the sunlight into the stables.

"Hush!" Heidi whispered. She was stroking the neck of a small brown-and-white pony whose shaggy mane fell over his dark eyes. "Apache didn't like his injection, did you, boy?"

"Aw! But it'll make you feel better," said Eva, scratching Apache's nose. Quietly, she went up to the other pony, a skinny chestnut named Rosie. "Do you want a pat too?" she murmured.

Rosie nuzzled Eva's palm with her soft nose. Inside the stall, a hay net hung from the wall, and there was a bucket of feed on the floor.

"We'll make you big and strong soon!" Eva promised, remembering the parched field where they had found her. A neighbor had called Animal Magic to say that the poor creature had been abandoned by her owners and left without fresh water while they took a two-week vacation in Spain.

"Hey, Apache," Heidi whispered, still stroking the little piebald. "That needle didn't really hurt, did it?" She turned to Eva. "Did you want something?" she reminded her.

"Oh, yeah. We've finished the flyers about the Open House. I wanted to ask if I can deliver them around town."

"Let me see."

Eva handed her mom a flyer. Heidi read through it, nodding, and finally said, "Yes, that's fine. It looks very good. Eva, did you hear me?"

"Hmm?" Eva had her arms around Rosie's neck, and she was murmuring sweet nothings into the pony's ear. "Oh, yeah. Thanks, Mom!"

Heidi smiled. "Go!" she urged.

"Okay, I'm out of here!" Eva said. "Here I come, Okeham!"

Chapter Two

Eva hurried up Main Street, pushing flyers into mailboxes, humming as she went. She felt really excited about Saturday. All the plans were going well, especially since Jake Adams had agreed to be there.

"Hi, George. Are you coming on Saturday?" she called to Karl's best friend, who straddled his bike in his driveway. She waved a flyer under his face. "You'll get to meet Jake Adams if you do!"

"Wow, no way! Is this for real?"

Eva nodded. "So you'll come?" She was already on her way.

"Count me in," George said. He cycled after Eva to the house next door. "What time does Jake arrive?"

"Two o'clock!" she called over her shoulder. "Be there early if you want to get his autograph!"

"Our big day will be here soon!" Eva told Treacle, Snap, and Wilma, one of four litters of kittens in the cat kennels. Charlie was their brother, and the only one so far to find a perfect new home.

"We'll have to make you look especially beautiful on Saturday," she cooed, lifting out ten-week-old Treacle and tickling his tummy.

The brown tabby wriggled and squirmed.

"Yes, I know, you're already adorable!" Eva laughed. Her dad had found the litter in an air vent at the back of a factory. Realizing that they were wild and that their mother was nowhere to be found, he had brought them right back to Animal Magic. Eva had named the four kittens before Jake Adams came along and took Charlie.

"There'll be hundreds of people," she promised, putting Treacle back into the kitten unit, then moving on to check a Siamese stray named Satin. Right now the cat area was bursting at the seams with animals needing owners, just like the dog kennels next door.

"Hundreds of people!" Eva repeated as she closed the door and went next door to see Penny, Bruno, and Becks. "Down, Becks!" she said sternly to the black Great Dane.

Becks, almost as tall as Eva, was a gentle giant who had been left at their door a month earlier. He gazed at her with soft brown eyes that would melt the hardest heart.

"*Hundreds!*" she promised, going from one kennel to the next.

The dogs woofed and whined. They jumped up and wagged their tails.

"People will line up for Jake Adams's autograph, then they'll come visit you," she told them. "They'll see you and fall in love with you. Before you know it, they'll want to take you home."

"Woof!" the dogs replied. "Woof, wruff, woof!"

Eva looked up at the pink sky as the sun disappeared in the west. "It's going to be the best, *best* day!"

Chapter Three

"Hi, Eva. Can I come in?" Annie Brooks poked her head around the door to the cat kennel.

It was early Friday morning, and Eva was feeding the cats. "Sure. Why not?"

Annie bit her lip nervously. "I wondered if you were still talking to me, after what Mom and Dad have done."

Eva smiled. "We're not at war with you, Annie. Only your mom and dad!"

"I'm so sorry!" Annie sighed. She walked

to the kitten unit, where Treacle, Snap, and Wilma snoozed in the warmth. "You know what Mom's like. She's always joining committees and setting up campaigns against stuff. Last year it was to stop cars from speeding through town."

"And this year it's to close us down," said Eva. "But why doesn't she like us?" she asked, placing a bowl of food in front of a white cat named Libby. Libby's long coat had been so filthy and matted that Heidi had decided to clip it off, except for the fur on her face and tail. Now she looked strange and scrawny as she gobbled her food.

Annie shrugged. "She thinks you're noisy and attract too much traffic, stuff like that."

"Doesn't she care about animals?"

"Yes, she does. She doesn't like having

them next door, that's all." Annie wanted to change the subject, so she asked if she could pick up Wilma.

"Go ahead," Eva told her. "With any luck, by this time tomorrow she might not be here!"

Annie nestled the tiny kitten against her. "So cute!" she murmured. Wilma meowed and cuddled up close. "Have they found you a new home?"

"Not yet. But our Open House is tomorrow, so here's hoping!"

Annie frowned and put Wilma back into the unit. She flicked her long blond hair behind her shoulders. "What Open House?"

"Oh," Eva said, feeling embarrassed. "Hmm, yeah. I was too scared to put a flyer into your mailbox," Eva said. "I thought your mom might yell at me. Anyway, we're inviting the whole town to Animal Magic so they can see what we do. Mom says it'll help find new owners for the animals."

"Hmm." Annie's frown deepened. "That means lots of cars and lots of people. Maybe I'd better break the news to Mom."

"Okay, if you think that's best," Eva said. "But poor you!"

"Yeah. I'd better go," Annie decided, heading for the door.

"Take a break," Heidi suggested when she saw Eva pushing a wheelbarrow toward the manure heap at the back of the yard. "Don't wear yourself out. It's going to be a long day."

"I'm fine!" Eva insisted, moving on. "I want to finish mucking out."

Her mom waited at the stable door until Eva came back with an empty wheelbarrow. "Good job!" she smiled. "I just came to take a look at Apache, to make sure he's okay after yesterday's shot."

"Apache's fine," Eva said, following Heidi into the stables. "But take a look at Rosie. She's stomping around and pawing the ground. She doesn't look very happy."

Heidi nodded. She looked at the little chestnut mare, who had now gone down onto her knees and was trying to roll onto her side inside her stall. "This doesn't look good," Heidi muttered, clicking into action. "Eva, bring me a halter. We need to get Rosie out of here and walking around the yard as quickly as possible."

Eva did as she was told. "What is it? What's wrong?" She held open the stable door as her mom buckled the halter, got the pony back on to her feet, and led her outside.

"It could be colic," Heidi replied. "If we've caught it early, she'll be okay."

Eva gasped and caught up with her mom. "And if not?" she asked.

"Colic is serious." Heidi didn't hide the facts. "If we haven't gotten to her in time, I'm afraid Rosie could die!"

"Poor Rosie!" Karl exclaimed. He had seen what was happening from the kitchen window and had run out to help. He took over the reins from Heidi, who ran to get her vet's bag from the clinic.

Eva felt helpless as she watched the pony stiffen her legs and refuse to walk. Then Rosie turned her head toward her flank and curled her lip to show her teeth. "Mom, hurry. She looks as if she's in real trouble!"

Heidi ran back. She checked Rosie's symptoms. "Yes, she's sweating, and her heart rate is racing. I'm pretty sure this is colic."

"Come on, girl," Karl urged.

"It's probably due to her change in diet," Heidi told them. She pressed her hands against Rosie's flank. "Yes, it feels like there's some kind of intestinal blockage. But if we keep walking her, it might clear up by itself."

"Walk!" Eva begged.

"Yes. Come on, Rosie, you can do it!" Karl urged.

Gamely, the little pony responded to their voices. She took a step forward, then another. Gradually, she began to move around the yard.

"Good work!" Heidi told Karl and Eva. In an emergency she always stayed calm.

"Eva, keep talking to her. Karl, keep some pressure on the reins to keep her moving."

"Does it hurt a lot?" Eva asked Heidi, who nodded. "It'll be better soon," Eva said to soothe Rosie.

"We hope!" Karl muttered.

Walking ahead of Rosie, Eva checked over her shoulder to see that the pony was still following. Out of the corner of her eye, she noticed Linda Brooks appear at the main gate. "Uh-oh!" she warned the others. "Here comes more trouble!"

"Everything okay?" Mark asked Eva. He'd called home during his lunch break. "Are we all ready for the big day?"

"Um, actually, not so good," Eva told him. "Rosie's got colic. Karl and I are taking turns walking her around the yard."

"Oh, no. How is she?" Her dad sounded worried.

"A bit better. Mom says it's probably food blockage, so hopefully it's not going to be serious long-term. Her temperature's going down now."

"Good. What else?"

"Mrs. Brooks came over."

"Uh-oh!" Mark knew this could only mean one thing. "What happened?"

"Annie told her about our Open House. Mrs. Brooks got really angry and yelled at

Mom. Mom kept her cool and said she was busy with an emergency. Mrs. Brooks said she'd call the police if cars blocked her driveway. She stomped around a bit, and then she went home."

"Oh, dear," Mark said. "Maybe I'll go over and see them when I get home from work."

"One more thing," Eva added, to top off what had been a bad morning. "Karl listened to the weather forecast and it's not good. They say there's going to be a thunderstorm tomorrow and heavy rain."

"Just what we need!" There was a long silence, and then her dad gave a deep sigh. "Never mind. Maybe things aren't going according to plan," he said. "But at least we still have Jake Adams up our sleeves!"

"Don't give Rosie anything to eat until I say so," Heidi told Eva before heading back to the clinic. A stray dog had just been brought in by one of the Animal Magic volunteers, and it needed a full examination. "She can drink plenty of water, but no food!"

Eva nodded and stroked Rosie's nose. The sick pony was back in her stable, still shaking from the pain of her colic. But her temperature and pulse were normal. She was over the worst.

"Good girl!" Eva soothed as Rosie nuzzled her hand. "You're going to be fine."

Eva settled the pony into her fresh, clean stable. "*We're* going to be fine!" she told herself, getting over the morning's events. "Dad will straighten things out with Mr.

and Mrs. Brooks. The forecast will be wrong, and tomorrow will be a lovely, sunny day. There'll be a huge crowd! And Jake Adams will be the star attraction!"

"I wouldn't count on it if I were you." Karl had wandered into the stable. There was a deep frown on his face.

"Uh-oh, it's Mr. Grumpy!" Eva told Rosie. "Seems like he's in a bad mood. Don't pay any attention."

Karl sniffed and went to stroke Apache.

"He gets like this," Eva explained brightly, as if Rosie understood every word. "Something probably went wrong with the Web site. Maybe he can't download a picture, or perhaps he's deleted something by mistake."

Karl's mood darkened. "Be quiet, Eva!"

She made a face behind his back. Then she felt bad for teasing him. "Okay, okay, I'm sorry. Is something really wrong?"

He sighed, turned away and then came back toward her. "We got a message from Jake Adams," he told her.

Eva's heart did a little flip and seemed to stop and then start again. "Saying what?" she whispered.

Karl looked her in the eyes and gave her the bad news. "Saying he can't come to the Open House," he reported. "Something happened. He had to go away."

Eva gasped. She shook her head in disbelief.

"It's true," Karl insisted. "It's all off. Jake won't be here tomorrow. *Finito*. End of story. *Kaput*."

Chapter Four

"Jake didn't give a reason," Karl insisted, shaking his head in disbelief. "He just said he had to go away. I can show you the e-mail if you want. I tried to send him a reply, but it just bounced back."

"No reasons and no apology?" Mark checked. He'd come home early to lend a hand with the preparations. "I'm really surprised. I thought Jake Adams was a decent guy."

"Me, too," Karl said gloomily.

"So now we have no celebrity." Heidi sighed. "And it's too late to find someone else or to let people know."

Eva sat without saying a word. Mrs. Brooks was on the warpath, it was going to rain, and now Jake couldn't come. Their big day lay in ruins.

"Maybe we should cancel the whole thing," Karl muttered.

"No, no, we have to go ahead," his dad argued. "Remember that our aim is to find new homes for our animals. It's a huge shame Jake's not coming, but people will still be able to look around the place, and we can still match up pets with new owners."

"But it *won't* be the same!" Karl insisted. "Everyone will be disappointed. What am I going to tell George when he shows up expecting to get Jake's autograph?"

"Dad's right," Heidi cut in. "We have to go ahead. Mark, do you want to go next door to calm Linda down, or shall I?"

Eva's dad got up from the table and headed for the door. "I'll do it."

Eva turned to Karl, who was still moping. "I want to look at Jake's e-mail. Can I use the computer in your room?"

"Feel free." He followed Eva upstairs and quickly went online.

Eva frowned as she read the message.

From: Jake Adams

To: Animal Magic

Subject: Open House

Message: Can't come tomorrow.
Have to go away. Jake.

She pressed the reply button and wrote, 'Can Marietta still make it?' Then she pressed Send. The message stayed in the outbox, then came back unsent.

"See!" Karl sighed. "Anyway, what's the point?"

"Marietta would be better than no one," Eva replied. "She gets in all the celebrity magazines. She's always going to parties with famous people."

Karl nodded. "But if we can't send an e-mail, we're stuck."

Eva frowned. She wasn't giving up that easily. She headed downstairs and into the yard. "No, we're not!"

"What are you doing? Where are you going?" Karl watched her grab her bike.

"I'm doing what people did before they had e-mail. I'm going to ride over to Okeham Hall and speak to Marietta!"

Karl's mouth dropped open. "Hey, wait! No, hang on!" He ran for his own bike and followed Eva to Main Street.

"I'm coming, too!" Karl called after her. "Eva, wait for me!"

Chapter Five

"O-o-oh, wow!" Karl stopped beside Eva at the gates of Okeham Hall. Karl had never seen the house before, even though he knew, like the rest of the world, that Jake Adams and his girlfriend had recently moved in.

The soccer star's home was fairy-tale stuff—a massive old house with a long, tree-lined drive. It had square towers and big stone pillars. "Where's the swimming pool?" he asked.

"Around the back," Eva told him. "Marietta gave Dad and me a quick tour when we came to drop off Charlie."

Karl got off his bike and propped it against the wall. He inspected the fancy iron gates. "These gates are electronic, and they're locked. What do we do now?"

"Press that button and speak into the microphone thingy?" Eva suggested.

Karl pressed, but nothing happened. "Looks like there's no one home. Come on, let's go."

"We're not going to give up that easily!" Starting to pedal again, Eva made her way cautiously along the road until she came to a narrow side path. "Come on!" she called.

The path was rough and overgrown, but, as Eva expected, it led along the side of the Okeham Hall property. A little way down she spotted what she'd been looking for.

"Look, there's a gate into the yard." Leaving her bike in some long grass, Eva went ahead and tested the handle. "And this one's open!"

She pushed the gate and stepped onto the soccer idol's smooth green lawn.

"Whoa, we could be in trouble here!" Karl pointed out. "This is trespassing."

Eva said, "I've been here before, remember? Marietta and Jake know me!"

Swallowing hard, Karl followed his sister across the wide lawn and then past a bright blue outdoor pool.

Eva led the way toward a door at the back of the old house and rang the bell. Once again, there was no answer.

"Look, they've both gone away," Karl insisted, turning to go. "We're wasting our time. Come on."

"They can't both have gone," Eva protested. "What about Charlie?"

Karl shrugged. "What *about* Charlie?"

Eva peered through the glass panels of the door. "He just came here. They wouldn't leave him home alone."

"Maybe a neighbor is looking after him. Come on, Eva, let's go!"

As Eva kept peering into the house, Karl turned to see a small orange shape peek out from behind one of the large flowerpots beside the door.

"Uh-oh!" he said, watching the fluffy kitten emerge from his hiding place. Charlie had a cute little face and two white paws. "You shouldn't be outside by yourself!"

Eva spun around and spotted him. "So much for him being looked after by a neighbor!" she muttered.

Scared and alone, the kitten began to run. He darted between more flowerpots, charging helter-skelter toward the swimming pool.

"Oh, no!" Eva saw the danger and began to run after Charlie. She tried to cut him off, but he scooted between her feet, under a poolside chair, and *splash*, right into the deep end of the pool!

Eva cried out as she watched poor little Charlie sink beneath the surface.

A split second later Karl was racing

toward the pool. He plunged after the kitten fully clothed.

Eva squeezed her eyes shut, hardly daring to watch. When she opened them again Karl had already caught hold of Charlie, pulling him back to the surface and holding him clear of the water.

"Here!" he yelled at Eva. "Grab him!"

She knelt and leaned out over the water to take the dripping kitten. "Are you okay?" she asked Karl.

"Yes, don't worry about me. How's Charlie?"

The kitten meowed and shivered in her arms. Eva took off her jacket and quickly wrapped him in it. "He'll be fine."

As Karl hauled himself out of the pool, Eva rubbed the kitten dry. She felt his rough little tongue lick her hand and saw his bright green eyes peer out from the folds of her jacket. "Don't worry," she murmured. "You're safe now."

"And I'm dripping wet!" Karl groaned, taking off a sneaker and emptying the water from it. "Honestly, Eva, I wish we'd never come!"

"Hush!" she told Charlie as he meowed and licked. "It's a good thing we came."

"Yeah, so we could scare the poor little thing and make him jump into the pool! Like that was a really good thing!"

Eva sighed. "Look, there's no cat door. If we hadn't come, Charlie would have been locked out and left all by himself. He could have fallen into the pool anytime, and no one would have been around to rescue him!"

"Yeah, I see what you mean." Karl grunted, putting his shoes back on.

"How could Jake and Marietta leave

him?" Eva said. "What were they thinking?" She made up her mind about what they had to do and began to head back the way they'd come. "We can't leave Charlie here. We'll have to take him back to Animal Magic."

Shaking his head like a dog drying itself, Karl ran after her. "Hang on! Let's just think this through."

But Eva didn't hesitate. "I'm not leaving Charlie home alone!" she insisted. "I don't care who Jake Adams is or what he says. Charlie is coming back with us!"

Chapter Six

"So now we have the mystery of the vanishing soccer star *and* the home-alone kitten on our hands." Heidi had taken Rosie's temperature and checked her pulse. Both were back to normal, and the pony stood comfortably in her stall.

"How could we have been so wrong in the first place?" Eva wondered. She stood with Charlie snuggled inside her jacket, fast asleep.

She and Karl had carried Charlie back

from Okeham Hall and told their mom what had happened. Heidi had sent Karl inside the house to change into dry clothes.

"We followed our Animal Magic rules, and we all thought Jake and Marietta were the perfect owners for the perfect pet!" Eva pointed out.

"We can't be right one hundred percent of the time," her mom said. "Hello again, little cutie," she murmured, tickling Charlie's chin. "I hear you've just used up one of your nine lives!"

"But Mom, you said Jake seemed to love cats," Eva reminded her. "Marietta, too. You said she wanted to take the whole litter home!"

Taking Charlie from Eva, Heidi led the way out of the stables toward the cat kennels. "People sometimes promise things, but don't act on their promises. They mean well at the time, I suppose."

Heidi popped Charlie into the kitten unit that housed Treacle, Snap, and Wilma. "Say hello to your brother!" she said with a smile.

The boldest of the kittens was Treacle, and he came forward to greet Charlie by sniffing and raising his front paw.

Charlie meowed and backed away, right into Snap, who rolled onto his back, paws in the air. Then Wilma pounced on Charlie and began to play fight.

"Wilma loves you, really!" Eva laughed as Charlie entered into the rough-and-tumble fray.

"The question is, are we going to let Charlie go back to Okeham Hall?"

"No way!"

Heidi gave Eva a serious look. "Not even if there's a good explanation?"

"Nope." As far as Eva was concerned, Jake and Marietta could never come up with a good enough reason to explain why they'd abandoned Charlie.

Before Heidi could reply, they heard Mark calling for her from the yard.

"With the cats!" Heidi called back.

Eva's dad joined them. "I just got back

from the Brookses' place," he muttered, a dazed look on his face.

"That was a long visit," Eva pointed out.

Mark scratched his head. "Yeah, I don't know what happened. I went to explain about our Open House, and before I knew it Linda Brooks was offering me coffee and Jason was going through all his old soccer scrapbooks with me."

"How come?" Eva asked.

"Does this mean peace has broken out?" Heidi said at the same time.

"Linda found out about Jake Adams being our star guest tomorrow," Mark explained. "Don't ask me how—she just heard it through the grapevine. Anyway, she told Jason, and it turns out Jason is a huge fan."

"But—" Eva tried to interrupt.

Her dad cut her off. "I know, but listen.

As soon as Jason heard that he could get to meet his idol, he convinced Linda that our Open House was a good thing because it would mean lots of our pets would find new homes, and so this place would be a lot less crowded and noisy. Which means it'll be quieter for them in the near future."

"But—" Eva tried again.

"I know, can you believe it?" He sighed and spread his hands, palms up. "They said they might even stop over tomorrow to see Jake."

"But Jake isn't coming!" Eva pointed out at last.

Her dad frowned. "I know. But I couldn't get a word in, and in the end I just didn't have the heart to tell them!"

Chapter Seven

"So what's going to happen to you?" Eva asked Charlie when she went to visit him later that evening.

Charlie was snuggled up next to Treacle, curled into a soft ball with his white front paws tucked under his chin. The tip of his orange tail twitched as Eva leaned in to pet him.

"It's okay, I won't disturb you," she murmured. "I'm just wondering what'll happen now. I hope Mom doesn't let you go back to Jake's place. I hope she lets us find you someone new."

Charlie closed his bright green eyes, and he dozed off.

"But if they do send you back, you have to promise not to go for another swim!" Eva said. "Remember, water and cats don't mix!"

Next to Charlie, Treacle opened his mouth and yawned. Over in the corner of the unit, Wilma and Snap were already fast asleep.

"Water—nasty, cold, wet stuff!" Eva insisted. "Brrr!"

Charlie opened one eye, then closed it again.

"Okay, I'll let you get some sleep." Eva smiled, giving him one last stroke. There were so many problems to solve and questions hanging over the kitten's future, but now it was late, and everyone was tired. "Good night, Treacle," she said. "Good night, Charlie. Sleep well!"

"Sleep well, Eva," her dad said as he turned off the light.

Eva lay on her back, staring up at the ceiling. She wasn't sleepy at all. Her head was too busy worrying about Charlie and wondering why his new owners had let him down.

I don't get it! she thought over and over. Why would anyone adopt a kitten and then leave him home alone?

She remembered poor little Charlie hiding among the big flowerpots at Okeham Hall.

He must have been hungry! she thought. *And lonely and scared!*

When she finally drifted off, her sleep was full of dreams about dark, glittering swimming pools and empty houses that had long, creepy corridors with creaking doors and spooky, whispering voices.

"Oh!" Eva woke up from her nightmare. She pulled her blanket tightly around her shoulders, gradually realizing that daylight was already filtering through her curtains. She breathed a sigh of relief.

Throwing back her blankets, she went to open the curtains. "Rain!" She groaned, peering out. The yard was covered in puddles, the slate roof of the clinic was shiny, and water trickled along the gutters. "What a rotten start to our Open House!"

Eva got dressed and went downstairs. She was halfway through her bowl of cereal before she looked at the clock and saw that it was only ten to six. No wonder no one else was up.

Okay, so what do I do now? she wondered. *Go back to bed? No, I know. I could send one last e-mail to Jake! Surely, it's worth a try.*

She pulled on her boots and raincoat and trotted across the yard to the clinic, where Joel Allerton was just finishing his night shift.

"What are you doing up so early?" Joel asked Eva. He yawned and ran his hand through his hair, checking off medicines on the shelf against a list on the computer screen.

"Couldn't sleep," she said, logging on to the computer next to Joel's. "Just wanted to send an e-mail!"

Click, click. Eva brought up yesterday's message from Jake and the one that she and Karl had tried and failed to send. 'Can Marietta still make it?' She tried again. Once more the mail server sent it back.

"No good," Eva muttered. She was over her disappointment and starting to get angry. "How come people you trust let you down?" she asked Joel.

"Which people?" Joel glanced at the screen. "Oh, you mean our local soccer

legend? I guess something important came up for him."

"*This* is important!" Eva insisted, pointing at one of the Open House flyers. "And so is adopting a kitten!"

"Ah, you mean Charlie." Joel had been keeping an eye on the orange tabby all night to make sure he'd settled back in with his brothers and sister. "I'm with you on that one!"

Eva nodded. "I want to know what's going on."

"We know what's going on," Joel pointed out. "Some big-shot sports star makes a spur-of-the-moment decision to adopt a cute kitten for his girlfriend. But a few days later she's bored with the kitty and they get invited to a friend's Spanish villa or whatever. Then it's bye-bye, Charlie, hello, sunbathing!"

Eva frowned. "It's so unfair!" she muttered, feeling even more angry. She jumped up from the computer, making her own on-the-spot decision. "If you see Mom and Dad, tell them I won't be gone long."

Joel glanced up from his monitor. "Why, where are you going?"

"Out!" Eva announced. "Back to Okeham Hall, to find out why Jake and Marietta abandoned Charlie!"

Eva bicycled through the rain. Drops fell from her helmet onto her cold cheeks. Her jeans were soon soaked through.

No traffic, she thought with relief, splashing through puddles. She noticed the wet black-and-white cows in the fields and a sad-looking horse poking its head over one of the hedges as she sped along the country road leading to the Hall.

But as she approached the wide gates, the morning silence was broken by the loud revving of a car's engine.

Eva braked and pulled into the grass on the shoulder of the road. The sound of the engine grew louder, and a small blue car shot out from Okeham Hall's driveway and headed toward her with a roar and a squeal of tires.

"Hey!" Eva cried, catching sight of a dark-haired woman at the wheel.

The woman sped past without seeming to notice her.

"Charming!" Eva muttered, her heart in her mouth. "*And* she didn't even bother to press the button and close the gates!"

As the sports car disappeared down the road, Eva seized her chance and rode

down the driveway toward the big house.

In the early morning rain the old house looked dark and spooky, just like the haunted house of Eva's dream. She could easily picture ghosts floating down corridors and appearing on the flat roof, gazing down from the eaves.

Get a grip! Eva told herself as she approached the wide front door. *And who was that woman in the blue car? It wasn't Marietta. And the car wasn't here when Karl and I came yesterday. What on earth is going on?*

Speaking of cars, Eva thought it would be a good idea to check the garage. "If Jake and Marietta are away, their cars won't be here," she said out loud, skirting down the side of the house to peer through the small windows of the old stables. To her surprise there were two cars parked inside. *Maybe they're back!* she thought.

She walked up to the front of the house and found the doorbell. *What now?* Eva wondered. Should she press it, or was it way too early to disturb Jake? Her finger hovered over the buzzer.

Then her gaze was drawn to a soggy piece of paper on the rain-spattered step.

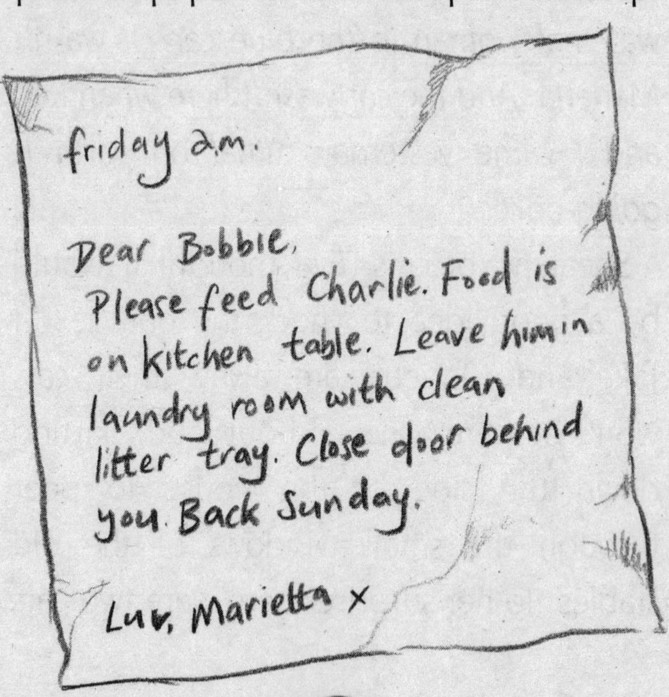
friday a.m.

Dear Bobbie,
Please feed Charlie. Food is on kitchen table. Leave him in laundry room with clean litter tray. Close door behind you. Back Sunday.

Luv, Marietta x

Eva stooped to pick it up. It was a smudged, hastily written message.

Eva's eyes opened wide. She smoothed the note and read it again.

So Jake and Marietta hadn't dumped Charlie after all. They'd made a plan to have him looked after by someone called Bobbie. But it had all gone wrong.

Bobbie hadn't turned up when he should have, and now Charlie was back at the rescue center. Which left two big questions in Eva's mind. Who was the woman in the blue sports car? And why was she in such a hurry to get away?

Chapter Eight

By nine o'clock, the yard at Animal Magic was buzzing with activity.

Eva watched people come and go. She had said nothing about her early morning visit to the Hall or the mysterious blue car that had shot out of the drive. She was still thinking about it when she saw a Land Rover splash through the puddles and enter the yard. She waved and ran to greet her grandpa.

"Have you come to help?" she asked as

Jimmy Harrison climbed out of the car. Eva grabbed him by the hand, steering him past the biggest puddles.

"You bet!" he grinned.

"What about Gro-well?"

Eva and Karl's grandpa ran a small garden center on the outskirts of town. You never saw him without his green gardening vest and a pair of sharp pruning shears stuffed in his pocket.

"I left Thomas in charge. He's been working for me long enough. I reckon he can manage by himself for one day." Still smiling, he waved at Mark and Karl. "When does the great man arrive?" he yelled. "Jake Adams is a real crowd-puller. Are you ready for the rush?"

Eva bit her lip. "Grandpa, didn't Dad tell you?"

"Tell me what?" Jimmy Harrison put on

his flat cap and zipped up his vest.

Eva broke the news bluntly. "Jake Adams isn't coming. He backed out at the last minute."

"Wow!" a voice from next door gasped. Annie's blond head appeared over the hedge. "Are you serious?"

Eva's shoulders sagged. "Jake can't come," she admitted. "Anyway, what are you doing, Annie? You're not supposed to listen to other people's conversations!"

"I can't help it if I happen to be in my yard!" Annie protested weakly.

"I'll leave you two to argue about it," Jimmy said, shaking his head and looking disappointed as he went off to find a job to do.

"You're *never* in your yard!" Eva tutted at Annie. "Especially when it's raining. You hate getting your hair wet!"

Annie ignored her. "What happened to Jake?"

"Don't ask me." Wiping the rain from her face, Eva realized it was no use being mad at Annie. "Sorry," she mumbled. "I know it's not your fault."

"No problem," Annie replied.

"Don't tell your dad," Eva pleaded. "He'll think we made it up—the stuff about Jake coming—just to stop your mom from complaining about us."

Annie nodded. "Okay, I won't say anything. But he's going to find out soon anyway—"

At that moment, there was a blast from a car horn in the driveway next door and the sound of tires squealing to a halt.

"Oops!" Annie turned in time to see her mom stop sharply at the end of their driveway.

Out of the corner of her eye, Eva saw a second car on Main Street. The driver jammed on the brakes. "That was close!" she said.

The second car swerved, then crunched into the lamppost outside Annie's house.

"Ouch!" Eva grimaced. She saw Karl sprint across the yard toward the road and she quickly followed. By the time they reached the gate, Linda Brooks was already out of her car and standing

on the sidewalk, while a dark-haired woman stepped shakily out of her small blue car.

"What do you think you're doing?" Linda shrieked. "This is a thirty-mile-per-hour zone! You must have been doing at least fifty!"

"Are you okay?" Karl asked the woman, seeing her front bumper bent around the lamppost and a hiss of steam emerging from under the hood of the car.

Soon other people came running, including Mark Harrison, who quickly took control. "Karl, go down the street and try to warn drivers that there's been an accident. Get them to slow down."

Karl nodded and hurried off. Eva stayed at her dad's side. She'd recognized the crashed car—it was the same one that she'd seen at Okeham Hall.

"Linda, are you okay?" Mark checked quickly, and then turned back to the other driver. "You've probably had a shock. Would you like to come inside while we try to straighten out your car for you?"

"Don't touch the car!" Linda insisted. "I'm going to call the police. They'll have

to measure braking distances before it gets towed away."

Sighing, Mark led the woman towards the house.

"I wasn't breaking the speed limit." The young woman spoke for the first time. "Your neighbor shot out from her driveway without looking. I had to swerve to avoid her."

Hearing this, Eva frowned. She'd seen how fast the woman had come out of the driveway at Okeham Hall a few hours earlier. But she didn't say anything.

"I'm so sorry to bother you," the woman continued, sitting down in the kitchen and accepting a cup of tea. "It looks as if I'm interrupting you on a busy day."

"No problem," Mark assured her. "Stay here. Eva will keep you company. I'll go outside and wait for the police."

Nodding, the woman took a deep breath and sipped her tea.

"Did you come to Okeham for any particular reason?" Eva asked carefully, her curiosity bubbling over in spite of the shock of the accident.

The woman looked pale and worried. She was young, with long glossy brown hair. "I went to my sister's house, but she wasn't in."

"Where does she live?"

The woman glanced cautiously at Eva. "It doesn't matter. Never mind."

She's hiding something! Eva thought. But there was no time to ask more questions, because her dad reappeared with a police officer who immediately asked to see the woman's driver's license.

"Roberta Jarvis," the policeman said, reading the name on the license and writing it down. "Now, Ms. Jarvis, how fast were you driving at the time of the accident?"

"Mom's gone nuts!" Annie reported to Eva an hour after the policeman had left. "She's denying coming out of the driveway without looking, and she's saying that Roberta Jarvis was going fifty!"

"Well, I heard Roberta tell the police that she was under the speed limit," Eva replied.

"Eva, can you check the hay in Rosie's and Apache's nets?" Heidi called from the clinic door.

Eva started toward the stables. "See you later," she told Annie. As she crossed the yard, her dad appeared at the back door with Roberta. He hurried over to Jimmy Harrison, who was helping Karl put up some streamers.

"Dad, could you give Roberta a lift?" he asked. "Her car's not running and she needs to get home."

"Of course." Jimmy smiled kindly at the pale young woman. "Where's home?"

"In Hareton," she explained with a hesitant smile. "I'm sorry to put you to all this trouble."

"No problem," he assured her. "It's only a couple of miles."

Hearing this, Eva dashed into the stable

to check on the ponies' feed and then hurried back out. "I'll go with Grandpa," she told her dad.

No sooner had she said this than Eva climbed into the backseat of the Land Rover with Roberta. Jimmy pulled out and switched on the radio.

"Sorry!" Roberta said again, seemingly on the verge of tears.

Jimmy drove past her wrecked car without replying.

"He didn't hear you. He's a bit deaf," Eva explained. "I saw you earlier," she said quietly.

Roberta shot her a worried look. "Where?"

Eva looked her in the eye. "At Jake Adams's place."

Roberta frowned. "Why were you snooping around there?"

"I was going to ask you that," Eva retorted. "Come on, you tell me first."

"I was looking for a cat." Roberta sighed. "A kitten, actually. It belongs to my sister."

It was Eva's turn to frown. "Marietta?"

Roberta nodded. "She and Jake had to go away suddenly."

"Marietta's your sister?"

"Yes. She asked me to take care of her kitten. But it escaped from the house and ran off."

Hang on a second! Eva tried to fit the pieces together. True, Marietta and Jake had had a sudden change of plans. But hadn't she found the note addressed to a man named Bobbie, asking him to take care of Charlie? That didn't make sense!

"I came to the Hall at noon yesterday," Roberta continued. "I only opened the back door a little way, and Charlie shot out between my legs and vanished!"

"Charlie!" Eva echoed. *Roberta. Bobbie. Bobbie's not a man—she's a woman!*

"I came back twice in the afternoon to look for him, but he never showed up," Bobbie explained. "And I got up early this morning and came over first thing. And again just after nine. Still no luck. Poor little Charlie has vanished into thin air. What am I going to tell Marietta when she gets back?"

Chapter Nine

"Grandpa, turn around!" Eva cried. She leaned forward and tapped his shoulder. "Take us back to Animal Magic, please!"

"Make up your mind," her grandpa grumbled.

Bobbie turned to Eva with a puzzled look. "What's up? Why are we going back?"

Eva took a deep breath. Suddenly, everything looked different. "There's been a big mistake!" she gasped. "Karl and I . . . we thought . . . well, anyway, you'll see!"

Jimmy Harrison turned the car around to go back to the rescue center.

"My brother and I wanted to find out why Jake had changed his mind about coming to our Open House," Eva told Bobbie. "He promised to be here, but then he backed out. That's why we went to Okeham Hall yesterday afternoon."

"Uh-oh. Eva, what have you been up to this time?" her grandpa asked.

"The house was empty and, well, we thought poor little Charlie had been left without anyone to look after him."

Bobbie nodded. "Okay, I get it. But actually, I was the one who messed up in the first place by letting Charlie escape. He ran off, and I couldn't get him to come back. I didn't know what to do!"

"Here we are, girls!" Jimmy announced, pulling into the yard at Animal Magic.

"Come on!" Eva urged Marietta's confused sister. She led her toward the cat kennels and headed straight for the unit containing Charlie and his brothers and sister. "Excuse me," she murmured to a couple of visitors who were gazing at the adorable litter. Then she leaned over and picked up the snuggly, fluffy orange tabby kitten.

"Charlie!" Bobbie gasped in total amazement. "Oh, Charlie, there you are! Thank heavens!"

"Am I in trouble?" Eva asked her mom as Bobbie cuddled Charlie.

Right away, Bobbie stood up for Eva. "Oh, please don't scold her! She did what she thought was best. And she saved Charlie from drowning, remember!"

"Actually, that was Karl," Eva admitted. Her brother hovered in the background, ready to bolt if things turned nasty.

"You're right, Bobbie." Heidi nodded. She reached out and patted Charlie. "All's well that ends well."

Phew! Eva relaxed and Karl came closer, smiling, hands in his pockets.

"Thank you so much!" Bobbie said to him. "You saved Charlie's life!"

"Do you happen to know why Jake had to cancel on our Open House?" Karl asked. "We're going to look really stupid when Mom has to make the announcement that he won't be here after all."

"I'm sorry, I really don't know." Bobbie, holding Charlie, walked with Heidi, Eva, and Karl out into the yard. There was a distant roll of thunder and heavy splashes of rain. Wet visitors ran to the cat kennels, and on into the converted barn that held the rabbits and guinea pigs. "I can't help you. I wish I could."

"Didn't Marietta tell you?" Eva persisted.

Bobbie shook her head. "Listen, can I call a taxi? I have to get Charlie back to Okeham Hall. And this time, I'll make certain he doesn't get out of the house!"

Eva's grandpa overheard and stepped forward. "No need for a taxi. I'll take you. As long as you don't change your mind again halfway there!"

No sooner said than Eva, Bobbie, and Charlie were back in the Land Rover and heading for the Hall.

"So Marietta didn't explain where she and Jake were going?" Eva prompted again.

"I thought it was a bit weird at the time," Bobbie confessed. "Marietta seemed upset when she phoned me and told me they had to go away. She wouldn't explain—just asked me to look after Charlie."

There was a short silence, and then Bobbie continued. "If you ask me, it had to do with the Angela Nixon fiasco."

"Who's she?" Eva asked.

"She is—no, she was until recently—Jake's personal assistant. She lived at the Hall with Jake and Marietta. But my sister found out on Thursday that Angela had been cheating on her expenses, and Jake fired her on the spot."

"But what's that got to do with Jake having to leave unexpectedly?" Eva didn't see it, and Bobbie had no real answers for her.

"I don't know—just a feeling," she murmured.

They lapsed into silence again as Jimmy turned into the driveway of Okeham Hall and drove slowly through the still-open gates toward the big old house.

"Home again!" Bobbie said to Charlie as she unlocked the front door.

The orange kitten sniffed and wriggled. Bobbie put him down gently and watched him stick his pointy tail straight up in the air and pad carefully across the polished floor.

"Meow!" Charlie said, heading for the kitchen.

"Maybe he's hungry," Bobbie said, inviting Eva and Jimmy into the house.

"Thirsty, more likely." Eva knew that the kittens had already been fed. She smiled to see Charlie lap greedily at the saucer of water that Bobbie put down.

Bobbie's phone rang, and she hurried to answer it.

"Marietta!" she said, walking quickly out of the kitchen and back into the hallway.

Eva couldn't hear what was being said, but she could tell that Bobbie sounded surprised. "Maybe now we'll find out what happened to Jake," she said glumly to her grandpa. They waited for Bobbie to return.

"I knew it!" Bobbie frowned, pacing up and down in the big kitchen. "It *is*

Angela Nixon! I knew she was bad news. Not only did she deliberately crash Jake's computer when she found out she'd been fired, she sent him off for a big meeting with United's boss that hadn't even been arranged!"

Eva's grandpa whistled gently. "Not Mark Moorcroft himself!"

Bobbie took a deep breath. "Yes, the big boss. Apparently, Angela said Moorcroft needed to talk to Jake about renewing his contract. She made it seem like his future on the team was in doubt and got him to drive all the way to United's headquarters, only to find there was no meeting after all. Moorcroft didn't show up, and it turns out he's on vacation with his family in Florida."

"Wow! That's mean!" Suddenly, a new thought flashed into her head. "Where are

Jake and Marietta right now?"

"On their way home."

"On their way home!" Eva echoed. "Wow, Bobbie, that's cool! Did they say . . . ? I mean, can you call them back? Find out if . . ."

With a smile, Jimmy stepped in to help out Eva. "I think what my excited granddaughter is trying to say is, will you ask Jake if he'll be back in time to put in an appearance at our Open House?"

Chapter Ten

It was after one o'clock when Eva and her grandfather arrived back at Animal Magic.

"Remember, don't say anything to your mom and dad about Jake," Jimmy reminded her, holding the car door open for Eva to jump out.

Back at the Hall, Bobbie had promised Eva that she would call Marietta back, but she warned them not to place too much hope on the celebrity couple being home in time. "I wouldn't want you to be disappointed all over again," she'd told Eva.

Even so, Eva's brown eyes were sparkling with excitement, and it was almost more than she could bear. *Jake, get here!* she begged silently. *Please get here! Everyone's still expecting you. Don't let us down!*

Meanwhile, visitors crowded into the yard. There was a buzz of conversation as people went from the dogs to the cats to the horses, and everyone was talking about the soccer superstar.

"Where's Jake Adams? He's not due until two . . ."

"It's good of him to support an animal rescue center."

"He must be a really nice guy!"

Eva followed a family of two parents and

two kids into the stables where Rosie and Apache munched hay.

"Look at the little brown pony, Mom!" the girl cried. "It says on the sign that her name's Rosie. How sweet!"

"Gorgeous," the woman agreed. "I had a pony just like her when I was your age."

Eva grinned and crossed her fingers. She moved on to the dog kennels, where a young couple were looking at Becks.

"Beautiful!" the woman said, and sighed, bending down to the Great Dane's eye level. "These dogs have lovely, gentle natures in spite of their size. Oh, Ben, wouldn't it be great to give Becks a home!"

Fingers crossed! Eva smiled and went on, past Penny's and Bruno's kennels. This could work out so well, if only Jake Adams could make it here in time!

"Hello, Eva!" Outside in the yard once more, she heard Annie's dad call her name. "Where's Jake? Is he here yet?"

Eva took a deep breath and said, "I don't know. Better ask Mom!" *Phew!* She breathed a sigh of relief as Jason dashed on. Then she spotted Annie hanging out by herself near the cat kennels.

"What a day!" Eva said, starting to tell Annie about Charlie. "He hadn't been left home alone after all! You know the woman in the blue sports car who ran into the lamppost? Well, it turns out she—"

"Stop!" Annie pleaded. She shook her head unhappily. "Didn't Dad tell you?"

"No. What?"

"About the accident. The police got back in touch. It looks like the woman in the blue car—"

"Bobbie," Eva interrupted. "Roberta, shortened to Bobbie."

"Yes, whatever. Well, it looks like she was going less than thirty miles an hour after all. And it was Mom who wasn't looking."

"Whoa!" Eva stared at her friend.

"I know. Mom's been crying. I guess she'll have to apologize to Roberta." Annie predicted that the next few days at home were going to be tough. "We don't know yet if the police will charge her."

"Wow!" Eva took a step back. "Hey, look, the sun just came out!"

"Just in time for me to make my announcement about Jake," Heidi muttered as she passed by with Mark. "I'm not looking forward to this!"

Eva glanced at her watch and saw that it was almost two o'clock. *Okay, I guess it was too much to hope for,* she told herself.

It would have been like a little piece of pure magic if Jake had shown up in time!

Still expecting the soccer star to appear through the door, the crowd of visitors gathered around. Eva spotted Jason Brooks and Karl's friend George Stevens along with a hundred other eager faces. This was the moment they had all been waiting for. "Oh, no, poor Mom has to tell them!" she groaned.

"Ladies and gentlemen, thank you for coming," Heidi began. "We're glad that so many of you have turned up to see the work we do here at Animal Magic."

Heidi smiled at the excited crowd and took a deep breath. "Unfortunately . . ."

But just as Eva hung her head, dreading her mom's next words, a car drove slowly into the yard and came to a halt.

All heads turned. The driver's door

opened, and Jake Adams stepped out.

A big cheer went up as everyone turned to greet the great man. Heidi Harrison stood outside her clinic door, wearing a look of stunned surprise.

Thank you! Eva clasped her hands together and jumped up and down on the spot.

"Jake, can I have your autograph?"

"Jake, write on this program!"

"Jake, you're the best striker United ever had!"

As the crowd swamped Jake Adams, Bobbie got out of the car with Marietta. They saw Eva and motioned to her. "You're a total star!" Marietta told her. "Bobbie told me everything you and Karl did for Charlie."

Eva grinned and blushed, unable to think of a thing to say. In any case, she saw that Jake had finally escaped from his fans and was standing by the clinic door, ready to make a speech. He looked shy and uncomfortable as he waited for the noise to die down.

"I just want to say what a great place this is," Jake began. "Heidi and her team are doing a wonderful job, and all the animals who end up at Animal Magic are extremely lucky. I just wish there were more centers like this one."

"Yeah!" Eva said, along with a lot of other people in the crowd.

"They need your support," Jake went on, "so now that you're here, why don't you stick around and adopt a pet, like we did? Go on, do it. Show that you care!"

"Great!" Eva cried, clapping loudly and then cheering as Jake disappeared inside the clinic. "We love you, Jake!" she yelled. "We so love you. We really do!"

Chapter Eleven

"We've found new homes for three rabbits and two guinea pigs," Mark said.

Karl clicked his mouse and brought up the details on the Animal Magic Web site. He put checks next to pictures of the pets who had been adopted.

"We also found owners for six dogs, including Penny, Bruno, and Becks," Joel reported.

"Wonderful!" Eva nodded happily. "And what about Rosie?"

"Maybe," Joel said. "It depends what we find out about her owners when they come back from their vacation. If it turns out the way we want it to, she'll go to the Boswells, because they can offer her a good new home."

"Cool." Their Open House had worked out perfectly, better than even Eva could have hoped.

"Best of all, we matched nine cats with new owners," Heidi told everyone. "Wilma and Snap both went to a ver, nice retired lady in town."

"Oh, poor Treacle," Eva whispered. "That means he's left here by himself."

Karl clicked and counted. "That's twenty-one animals altogether," he said. "How cool is that!"

"Twenty-two!" a voice said, and they all turned to see Bobbie, Jake, and Marietta

standing at the door of the office.

Karl counted again. "Three plus two plus six plus one plus nine. That makes twenty-one," he insisted.

But Bobbie came forward holding a squirming tabby kitten in her hands. "I'd like to adopt Treacle," she said with a smile. "If you think I'll be a good owner, that is."

Heidi looked at Eva. "What do you think?"

Eva went up to Bobbie and took Treacle from her. She cuddled him close. "I think you'll be perfect!" she said to Bobbie. She was sure Bobbie would care for him and feed him and keep him safe. "You know, Dad found him in an air vent behind a factory."

Bobbie, Jake, and Marietta listened to the whole story as Eva took Treacle out

into the warm sunshine.

"Dad works for a package delivery company. He was in the factory parking lot when he heard a meowing coming from an air vent, so he went to take a look. . . ."

Karl, Heidi, and Mark stood in the doorway watching Eva chatter to their guests.

"So cool!" Karl sighed, staring at Jake and suffering from a serious case of hero worship.

"A good day!" Heidi said, bringing out a cardboard pet carrier for the kitten. Animal Magic had done its job.

Eva popped Treacle into the carrier and took him over to Jake's car.

"He's been microchipped, and he's had his shots," Eva assured Bobbie. "You don't need to worry about that."

As Jake started the engine, Marietta leaned out the window. "Thanks, Eva!"

Eva nodded and smiled. Her dad came to join her and put his arm around her shoulder.

"Give me a call anytime you need me," Jake told him as he started the car.

As they watched the soccer star leave the yard, Eva looked up at her dad. "Okay,"

she said, her eyes sparkling and a grin splitting her face from ear to ear. "When do we have our next mega Animal Magic Open House?"

ANIMAL
RESCUE